SUMMER READING AWARD

in Honor of

REBECCA DEAN

1988

James Prendergast Library Association
509 Cherry Street Jamestown NY 14701

SiLLY BABY

by Judith Caseley

Greenwillow Books, New York

 Watercolor paints and colored pencils were used for
the full-color art. The text type is ITC Garamond.

Library of Congress Cataloging-in-Publication Data

Caseley, Judith.   Silly baby.
Summary: Lindsay does not welcome her new
baby sister to the family at first, but the realization
that she herself was once a similar
baby helps her change her mind.
[1. Babies—Fiction. 2. Sisters—Fiction] I. Title.
PZ7.C2677Si 1988   [E]   87-4097
ISBN 0-688-07355-7
ISBN 0-688-07356-5 (lib. bdg.)

TO JENNA,

MY

BUNDLE OF JOY

Mama looked in the mirror.

"Am I getting fat?" she asked Papa and Lindsay.

"No," said Papa. "I like you just the way you are."

"Me too," said Lindsay.

Mama shook her head and sighed.

Mama went to the doctor's for a check-up.
When she came home, she sat Lindsay on her lap
and said, "I'm going to have a baby. You're going
to have a brother or sister."

"No, thank you," said Lindsay.

Some mornings, Mama felt sick. She stayed in bed
and ate crackers. It made her feel better. Lindsay ate
crackers, too. Sometimes she ate cereal and milk.
"Just don't spill the milk," said Mama. "You're on
Papa's side of the bed."

Every day, Mama's stomach got a little bigger. One day, Mama took Lindsay's hand and put it on her stomach. Lindsay felt a tiny thump and a flutter.

"What's that?" she asked.

"That's the baby," said Mama, "floating in water in my stomach."

"Silly baby," said Lindsay.

Mama got very large. At story time Lindsay sat on
Mama's lap. But Mama's stomach was in the way,
and Lindsay had to get off.

One night, Papa and Mama woke Lindsay.
"Grandma's here," said Papa. "The baby is coming."
"Tell him to come next year," said Lindsay.
"The baby won't wait," Mama said. "Don't you want
 to see if you have a brother or sister?"
"No," said Lindsay. "I like things just the way they are."

In the morning, Lindsay painted a picture of the baby.
"Silly Baby," she wrote on it, and she hung it in the baby's room.

When Mama came home she showed Lindsay a tiny
bundle with very little hair.

"Here's Callie," said Mama.

"She's funny," Lindsay said. "She looks like Grandpa."

The baby cried.
"She's noisy!"
Lindsay shouted.
"She's brand-new,"
said Mama, "and
she has to exercise
her lungs."

"She's dumb!"
shouted Lindsay.
"Dumb, dumb, dumb!"

Mama hugged Lindsay.

"We have a new baby," said Mama.

"But you're our first baby."

Papa hugged her, too.

Callie cried and cried.
It was hard to sleep at night.
Mama walked her up and down.
She jiggled her.

The baby screamed.
Papa rocked her very fast.
Mama frowned at Papa
and took her, and rocked
her slowly.

"The baby has gas," said Mama to Lindsay.

"Cars have gas," said Lindsay.

 The baby cried some more. Mama wrapped
 her like a mummy.

"Crying is the only way a baby can talk,"
 said Papa.

"Silly baby," Lindsay said.

One evening, the baby wouldn't let them eat.
Mama held Callie with one arm and ate spaghetti
over her with the other. Some strands of spaghetti
fell on the baby.

"Messy baby," said Lindsay.

The next day, a large carton arrived in the mail.

Mama and Lindsay opened it up.

"It's a baby swing!" cried Mama.

"Another present for Callie," said Lindsay.

That evening, Papa set up the swing. He showed Lindsay
how to wind it up. Mama put Callie in the little seat.
Callie started to cry. Her tiny feet kicked. Her face got red.
Lindsay gave the swing a push, and it started. Click, click,
back and forth. The baby was quiet. The baby fell asleep.

They all ate supper as the baby rocked. Mama talked to Lindsay. Papa talked to Lindsay. The baby slept. After supper, Mama lifted Callie carefully out of the swing and put her to bed. The baby was quiet.

Mama and Papa and Lindsay went into the living room
and sat on the couch. Mama took out a big book.
Lindsay sat on Mama's lap and turned the pages.
"These are pictures of you," said Mama, "when you
were a baby."

Lindsay saw pictures of herself crying . . .

and dribbling . . .

and waving her arms . . .

and kicking her feet . . .

and wrapped up like a mummy.

"I was a silly baby, too!" said Lindsay.

"And look how smart you are now!" Papa said.

Lindsay smiled.

"Maybe Callie will be like me," she said.

Then they tiptoed into Callie's room.

Lindsay leaned over Callie's crib and kissed her,
very carefully, good night.

E
Caseley, Judith.   C-1
    Silly baby

                                11.95

DATE DUE		
FEB 17 1989		
2/27/90		